Hades and the
Helm of Darkness

HEROES IN TRAINING

Hades and the Helm of Darkness

Joan Holub and Suzanne Williams

Aladdin

NEW YORK LONDON
TORONTO SYDNEY NEW DELHI

This book is a work of fiction. Any references to historical events, real people, or real places are used fictitiously. Other names, characters, places, and events are products of the authors' imagination, and any resemblance to actual events or places or persons, living or dead, is entirely coincidental.

ALADDIN

An imprint of Simon & Schuster Children's Publishing Division
1230 Avenue of the Americas, New York, NY 10020
First Aladdin paperback edition April 2013
Text copyright © 2013 by Joan Holub and Suzanne Williams
Illustrations copyright © 2013 by Craig Phillips
All rights reserved, including the right of reproduction
in whole or in part in any form.
ALADDIN is a trademark of Simon & Schuster, Inc.,
and related logo is a registered trademark of Simon & Schuster, Inc.
Also available in an Aladdin hardcover edition.
For information about special discounts for bulk purchases,
please contact Simon & Schuster Special Sales
at 1-866-506-1949 or business@simonandschuster.com.
The Simon & Schuster Speakers Bureau can bring authors to your live event.
For more information or to book an event,
contact the Simon & Schuster Speakers Bureau at 1-866-248-3049
or visit our website at www.simonspeakers.com.
Designed by Karin Paprocki
The text of this book was set in Adobe Garamond Pro.
Manufactured in the United States of America 0313 OFF
2 4 6 8 10 9 7 5 3 1
Library of Congress Control Number 2012942890
ISBN 978-1-4424-5267-1 (pbk)
ISBN 978-1-4424-5725-6 (hc)
ISBN 978-1-4424-5268-8 (eBook)

For Ward Williams, best son ever —S. W.
For Paul, best brother ever —J. H.

⚡ Contents ⚡

Greetings,
Mortal Readers,

I am Pythia, the Oracle of Delphi, in Greece. I have the power to see the future. Hear my prophecy:

Ahead I see dancers lurking. Wait—make that *danger* lurking. (The future can be blurry, especially when my eyeglasses are foggy.)

Anyhoo, beware! Titan giants now rule all of Earth's domains—oceans, mountains, forests, and the depths of the Underwear. Oops—make that *Underworld*. Led by King Cronus, they are out to destroy us all!

Yet I foresee hope. A band of rightful rulers called Olympians will arise. Though their size and youth are no match for the Titans, they will be giant in heart, mind, and spirit. They await their leader—a very special yet clueless boy. One who is destined to become king of the gods and ruler of the heavens.

If he is brave enough.

And if he can get his friends to work together. And if they can learn to use their new amazing flowers—um, amazing *powers*—in time to save the world!

CHAPTER ONE
Stinky River Styx

Zeus, Poseidon, and Hades stood on a hill, gazing downward. A river wound like a snake through the gloomy valley below. It was all that stood between them and their goal—the Underworld.

Zeus sniffed the air, then wrinkled his nose. "P.U.! What is that stinky smell?"

Poseidon pointed toward the valley with the

three-pronged end of his trident. "I think it's that river."

The river looked brown and sludgy. There was a giant sign by it that read: RIVER STYX.

Maybe the sign was written wrong, thought Zeus. Maybe it should really say: RIVER *STINKS*!

Hades gazed happily at the river. "What are you guys talking about? I think it's awesome!"

"You would, weirdo," said Poseidon. "Well, you know what I think? I think there's no way I'm going near that river. I think that oracle is crazy."

Zeus knew he meant Pythia, the Oracle of Delphi. She'd sent them here to the Underworld on a quest. They were supposed to find the Helm of Darkness. Whatever that was. As usual, she hadn't fully explained. She always seemed to expect them to figure these things out on their own.

"But you like water, remember?" Zeus told Poseidon. He tried to sound more cheerful and encouraging than he felt. "I mean, you're an Olympian—the god of the sea!"

They'd discovered this on their last quest to the Aegean Sea. There they'd found Poseidon's trident in the possession of a Titan named Oceanus. The trident was like a pitchfork, only cooler. They'd found Hades in the sea too.

However, they'd also lost Hera. She'd gone looking for the trident on her own. Who knew where she was now? Zeus hoped she was somewhere safe.

"I like clean, blue rivers," Poseidon informed him. "Not stinky gloppy skunk water. Besides, it's not just the river that creeps me out. It's that whole place down there. It's so—"

Honk!

The boys looked around in alarm. Where

was that loud, deep honking sound coming from? Right then a sudden spurt of hot steam sprayed up out of the ground under Poseidon. He jumped a foot high.

"Steamin' undershorts!" he yelled, grabbing his behind with his free hand.

Honk! Psst! Another squirt of hot steam burst unexpectedly from the ground. This one struck Hades. *"Yeowch!"* He grabbed his behind and hopped around too.

Honk! Psst! Honk! Psst! More spurts gushed out of the ground.

Then one struck Zeus. He jumped in surprise and pain. "Thunderation, that's hot!"

"Let's get out of here!" Poseidon called. The boys ran toward the river.

Anytime they slowed, a honk sounded and another spurt of steam attacked. *Honk! Psst!* "Ow!" *Honk! Psst!* "Ow!"

"Last ferryboat to the Underworld!" shouted a voice up ahead. Zeus squinted his eyes at the boat. It was sailing toward them from the opposite side of the river. Since it was the same brownish color as the water, it blended in. That's why they hadn't noticed it before.

"A boat to the Underworld?" called Hades. "Perfect! Let's get on it."

"Like we have any choice?" Poseidon yelled back.

"Yeah," Zeus agreed breathlessly. "It's like we're being herded down to the boat." The spurts were chasing them, so they could only move forward.

And it wasn't just the three boys who were being rounded up. Dozens of other people began to appear. They streamed down the hill running for the boat too. Most of them were really old. But they were moving pretty fast.

As the boys got closer to the boat, they saw a man on board. He reached up to pull a string attached to a horn. Another loud honk sounded. More hot spurts shot out of the ground around them.

"Hey! I think that ferryboat horn is what's causing the steam to honk out," Zeus told his friends.

The three boys dashed the rest of the way to the ferry. Just as they were about to leap onto it, a hand blocked their way.

"Halt!" It was the man who had sounded the horn. He was pale, with long white hair and wrinkled skin. And he was wearing a hat with his name: Captain Charon.

He peered at them closely. "Are you dead?" he asked them.

Zeus nodded, breathing hard. "That's for sure. Dead tired. We could use a ride."

"No, I think he means—" Hades started to tell Zeus.

"All righty, then. Pay your fare," the captain interrupted. "Passage across the River Styx costs one obol. Each." He held out his hand, palm upward, waiting.

"Better pay the fee," a woman behind them advised. "It's either that or wander these shores for one hundred years."

"We don't have any money," Zeus admitted.

"Next!" said Charon, pushing the three boys aside. He let a man come forward. The man opened his mouth and stuck out his tongue. There was a silver coin on the tip of it!

Charon took the coin and flipped it high with his thumb. It arced through the air. *Plunk!* It landed in a coin bag tied at his waist.

"Get lost," Charon barked at the boys when they didn't leave. "You're blocking others who can cough up the fare. They're *dying* to get in."

Zeus and Poseidon just stared at him.

The ferryboat captain grinned. "That was a joke. Get it?"

"No," Zeus and Poseidon said at the same time.

But Hades burst out laughing.

Zeus and Poseidon looked at each other, not getting what was so funny.

"Finally," Charon said to Hades, sounding flattered. "Someone who appreciates a good joke. Are you with them?" he asked Hades, hooking his thumb toward Zeus and Poseidon.

Hades nodded.

"Okay, then. Just this once I'll overlook the fare. Welcome aboard!" Captain Charon stepped aside and waved the three boys onto his boat.

CHAPTER TWO
Wild Ride

Charon used a long pole to push the ferry-boat off the riverbank once everyone was aboard. As they began the trip back across the river, he smiled big.

"All righty, shades, you paid your obol. Now it's showtime!" he announced. "Let's see if I can bring a little *life* to this party!"

"Why is he calling everybody shades?" Zeus mumbled.

"Because that's what we are. Shadows of our former selves," explained the man standing next to him.

The boys stared at him, unsure what he meant. The others on board did look kind of pale, thought Zeus. But they were people, not shadows.

Just then Charon's voice boomed out, making everyone jump. "First a little humor. Who can tell me what the favorite game in the Underworld is?"

Before anyone could guess, Charon answered his question himself: "Pick-Up-Styx! Ha-ha-ha!"

The ship got dead quiet. Everyone looked confused.

Then Hades burst out laughing again. "Oh, I get it. You mean 'sticks,' which sounds like 'Styx.' Which is the name of this river. Ha-ha-ha! Good one!"

"Thanks. I got a million of 'em!" Encouraged,

Captain Charon proceeded to tell one joke after another. And he supplied all the punch lines himself without giving anyone a chance to guess them.

"What are the Greek gods' favorite musical instruments?" he asked. "Harp-ies."

"Why did the Greek student fail the test? Because he made too many mythtakes."

Zeus rolled his eyes. Poseidon groaned. Hades kept on laughing.

A man next to them leaned toward the boys. "Why did the shade beg the boat captain to stop telling lame jokes?" he asked. Then, just like Charon, he gave the punch line. "Because they were killing him—again."

Zeus looked at the man, still confused. Poseidon shrugged and said, "Whatever. But if his jokes don't kill us, the stink from this river probably will."

"I like Charon's jokes," Hades protested as the man turned away to talk to someone else. "And I still don't see what's wrong with the river."

The three boys looked over the railing. The muddy water below swirled with globby goop. Every now and then strange crocodiles with pink eyes surfaced to blink at them.

"It looks and smells like garbage stew," said Zeus.

"Yeah," Poseidon agreed. "Maybe I can clean it up with my trident, though. Like I fixed the sea on our last quest."

He stuck the tip of his gleaming golden trident into the mucky water. Then he stirred it around, chanting:

"Trident, trident—tried and true,
Turn this river sparkling blue."

After a few stirs the three boys gazed expectantly at the river. But it remained sludgy brown.

"Maybe your trident's powers don't work in the Underworld," said Hades.

Poseidon looked alarmed. "But they have to work! We can't go on a quest without magic. How will we defend ourselves?" He kept stirring and staring hopefully at the water. Nothing happened.

Now Zeus was worried too. He reached for his dagger-size thunderbolt and pulled it from his belt.

"Bolt! Large!" he commanded. But the zigzag bolt didn't sizzle or spark with electricity. And instead of expanding into a five-foot-long thunderbolt, it stayed the size of a small dagger.

Zeus and Poseidon shared panicky looks. Zeus had gotten used to having the thunderbolt's magic to help him out of bad situations.

He'd pulled the bolt from a magical stone in the temple of Delphi. Since then it had become a friend as well as an amazing weapon.

Friend? No! I shouldn't think of it like that, he thought. After all, the bolt didn't even belong to him. It belonged to some guy named Goose. The oracle had told him that. And as soon as Zeus found Goose, he was going to have to give him the bolt.

"Check your chip," Hades suggested. "See if it's working."

"Good idea." Zeus tugged on the leather cord around his neck. There was a smooth stone as big as his fist strung on the cord. He'd gotten it from the temple too. It was a magic amulet that could speak and give directions.

The three boys leaned in to study it.

"Chip?" Zeus asked it. But it didn't reply.

"No symbols," Poseidon noted. "No compass

arrow either. I think Hades is right. Our gadgets don't work here in the Underworld." He yanked at his trident. Its prongs had gotten tangled in some seaweed and wouldn't come loose.

"Which means we're doomed!" Hades moaned. Suddenly he didn't sound so cheery anymore. "We can't complete our quest without weapons or a compass to show us where to go. Remember what the oracle said?"

Zeus nodded, then quoted her from memory: "'You must find the Helm of Darkness. It rightfully belongs to the one who is lord of the Underworld. Find it and you will also find more of the persons you seek. Only, beware of the second of the king's Creatures of Chaos. For they are far more dangerous than—'"

Wham! Suddenly the ferryboat gave a hard jerk. Everyone on board stumbled and swayed. Zeus and Hades lost their balance and fell to their knees. Poseidon hung on to the railing with one hand and his trident with the other. Frightened cries sounded among the passengers.

Wham! The boat pitched forward again. "Those pink-eyed river creatures are snapping at my trident!" Poseidon shouted.

Each time the creatures missed, their flat, scaly noses hit against the boat's hull. That was what was causing the jerks.

"You—with the pitchfork!" yelled Captain Charon, pointing his river pole at Poseidon. "Don't tease the crockydeads!"

CHAPTER THREE

Three Rules

Wham! The boat shuddered yet again.

Chomp!

"Help! The crockydeads just sunk their teeth into my trident," Poseidon cried out in disbelief. "They're trying to steal it!"

Zeus jumped to his feet. He, Poseidon, and Hades all grabbed the trident's handle. They pulled hard. But the creatures were strong. They pulled back harder. It was a tug o' war!

Thump! The ferryboat bumped into the landing dock. They'd crossed the river and were on its far shore now. The jolt surprised the crockydeads into letting go of the trident. The three boys yanked it out of the river.

The crockydeads gave the boat one last slam with their snouts. Then they slithered away into the oozy brown water.

Captain Charon scowled at the three boys. "Troublemakers!" Using his ferryboat pole, he shoved them over to the gangplank. "Get off my boat!"

"Wait!" Zeus said. He grabbed the gangplank railing and stared at the captain. "Maybe this isn't the best time to ask, but my compass isn't working. I wonder if you could give us some directions before we go?"

"We're looking for the Helm of Darkness," added Poseidon.

Hades nodded hopefully. "Have you heard of it? We know it's here somewhere in the Underworld, but we don't know wh—"

Bam! Charon banged the end of his pole onto the deck, interrupting him. "There are three rules here in the Underworld."

He stepped toward them, wearing a fierce expression. Zeus, Poseidon, and Hades each took a step backward down the gangplank.

Charon held up a bony finger in front of their faces. "Rule number one: Don't ask nosy questions. Got it?"

The three boys nodded.

Charon took another step forward, and the boys each took another step backward. He held up two fingers. "Rule number two: Obey orders. Got it?"

The three boys nodded again.

"Good!" Charon gave them each another

sharp nudge with the long ferryboat pole. "Now get off this boat!"

"I wonder what rule number three is," Hades whispered to Zeus.

"Probably best not to ask," Zeus advised.

"Yeah, don't forget rule number one," said Poseidon.

The boys scuttled down the gangplank and hopped onshore. Other passengers swarmed past them in a hurry, sweeping them along. The ground was swampy and sucked at their sandals as they ran.

They were all heading for a fence a few dozen steps from the riverbank. It was made of iron spikes twice as tall as the boys. And it looked like it surrounded the entire Underworld!

Creeeak! Suddenly two giant gates in the middle of the fence magically swung open. Like the jaws of a giant sideways crockydead mouth, they looked ready to gobble everyone!

"Creepy," Poseidon muttered as they entered.

"You mean awesome!" Hades exclaimed.

"Why does this gate's magic work in the Underworld but ours doesn't?" Zeus wondered aloud. His companions were too busy studying their surroundings to answer.

"Look!" Poseidon said after they passed through the gates. He was pointing to something ahead. A magnificent golden throne! It was just sitting there in the middle of the swamp. Empty. Except for a square jeweled box that rested upon its velvet seat.

A big sign hung on the back of the throne. It read: BEWARE OF THREE-HEADED DRAGON DOG.

Hades had been pretty delighted with everything about the Underworld so far. But suddenly he screeched to a halt.

"Dog? Three-headed *dragon dog*?" His eyes

widened in fear. "I'm outta here!" He spun around and fled toward the gates and the riverbank.

"Come back! We need to stick together," Zeus called out. When Hades didn't stop running, Zeus and Poseidon chased after him.

The tall spiked iron gates were slowly swinging shut now that everyone was inside the fence. Beyond them the boys could see Charon angling his long pole against the shore of the River Styx. He pushed off.

"Wait for me!" Hades shouted to him. He put on a burst of speed, trying to make it through the gates in time.

CLANK! The gates swung shut in his face.

Hades grabbed on to two of the tall iron rails and stuck his face between them. "Take us with you!" he yelled toward the ferryboat.

Charon glanced back at the three boys. His ferry had already begun to cross the river toward the opposite shore. "No can do. Remember rule number three?"

The boys shook their heads. "No! You didn't tell it to us!" yelled Poseidon.

Charon shrugged. "Rule number three is: This ferry only carries passengers one way—*into* the Underworld. Once you're in, you're in. There's no escape."

Which meant they were all stuck in the Underworld—forever!

Grrr! Grrrowl! The three boys whipped around at the threatening sounds.

A snarling, drooly dog had appeared way behind them by the throne. The dog was scaly like a dragon and almost as big as the Delphi temple! It even had a dragon's tail that ended in a sharp arrowhead-shaped point. Besides that it had three heads! And each one was growling.

The three boys stood frozen at the sight.

"We're trapped!" wailed Hades.

"With no magic!" moaned Poseidon.

"C'mon," said Zeus. "We're sitting ducks out here by ourselves. Let's go mingle with the others before that dog notices us."

Quickly they made their way into the middle of the group. "We are *so* dead!" Hades muttered.

"True," said a man alongside him. "I was struck down in a battle a week ago." He drew a finger across his throat.

"I tripped over a bucket and broke my neck," said another man. "Kicked the bucket, you might say."

"Snakebite," said a third guy. "Never recovered."

"What are you guys talking about?" asked Zeus.

"How we bit the dust," the snakebite guy said matter-of-factly.

"You mean to say that you're all *dead*?" asked Poseidon. He'd finally put two and two together.

"Of course," said Hades. "That's what Captain Charon's jokes were about. Duh—didn't you get it?"

The others nearby in the crowd nodded.

Poseidon stared at Zeus and Hades, terrified. "*We're* not dead, though. Are we?"

"No way!" said Zeus, trying to calm him.

Then he had an awful thought. The oracle had promised they'd find *more of those they sought* here in the Underworld. Which meant more Olympians. But he'd also hoped it meant he might find his mom and dad—whom he couldn't even remember. His mom had left him in a cave in the care of a nymph, a goat, and a bee when he was just a baby.

But if everyone down here was already dead,

did that mean his parents were dead too? His heart sank.

Still, he tried to be brave for the sake of his two friends. "Don't worry. I didn't go to all that trouble to free you for us to end up dead!" he assured them.

Poseidon and Hades were two of the five Olympians he had rescued not long ago. They'd been trapped in the belly of Cronus, the big bad king of the Titans. With a toss of his thunderbolt down the king's throat, Zeus had made Cronus barf them all up. Now Zeus felt kind of responsible for them. At the end of this quest they just *had* to get out of here alive!

Except for a few growls now and then, it had gone quiet around them. The boys peeked from the crowd to see what was going on.

"That dog is herding everybody into three lines," said Poseidon.

There was a sign at the front of each line. Zeus squinted to read them all. "The sign on the left has a big *E* on it," he reported. "The middle sign has an *A*."

"The one on the right has a *T*," added Hades.

"E-A-T spells 'EAT'," said Poseidon.

Zeus cocked his head. "Eat?"

"I knew it!" wailed Hades. "That dragon dog is dividing us up into his breakfast, lunch, and dinner!"

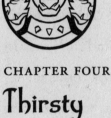

CHAPTER FOUR

Thirsty

Hades' loud wail reached the dog's three sets of ears. Its three heads bobbed up. Its six red eyes narrowed, scanning the crowd.

"Looks like we're not so safe mingling with the crowd after all," said Zeus. "Let's get out of here."

"I'm with you," said Poseidon, peeling off from the line.

"Hey, wait for me!" called Hades. Ducking

behind some shades, the three boys tried to sneak off into the nearby bushes.

Woof! Woof! Woof!

"Oh, no!" yelped Hades. "He's spotted us!"

Sure enough the dragon dog came bounding over, all three heads snarling and drooling. In an instant the beast had the boys cornered.

Hades tried to run past it. But he tripped over a scaly log. The dog growled and leaned over him, baring three sets of teeth.

"Get away!" Hades shouted. Half-sitting on the log, he felt around for a weapon. His hand wrapped around something. A stake! Using both hands, he yanked it from the log. Maybe he could use it to defend himself.

Oww-ooo! The dog started howling. It tucked its tail between its front paws.

Suddenly the log was gone and Hades was sitting on the ground. He looked down at the

stake in his hand. It was actually a thorn. A very large thorn.

"Thunderation! You just pulled that thing out of the dragon dog's tail!" said Zeus.

"Tail?" echoed Hades. "I thought it was a log!"

"Run!" called Poseidon.

Before Hades could budge, the dog's heads whipped close. Three mouths opened, each showing two rows of icicle-sharp teeth.

Zeus gasped, sure that Hades was a goner.

Then the dog let out a gurgle that sounded sort of like, "Sir. Brr. Us." Its three tongues slipped out. *Lick! Lick! Lick!*

"Stop! Eew!" yelled Hades, swatting at the dog's heads. "Help! It's licking me to death!"

"No way I'm sticking around to be dragon dog dinner!" said Poseidon. Arms and legs pumping, he took off for the bushes.

Zeus grabbed Hades' arm and pulled him up. The two boys followed Poseidon.

"Is it after us?" Hades asked after they'd gone a dozen steps.

Zeus had been sure the dog would give chase. Glancing over his shoulder, he saw that it hadn't, though. In fact, it was just sitting there holding its tail and staring after Hades. It looked kind of sad, like its feelings were hurt.

Weird. But before Zeus could think much about it, he stumbled over a tree root. He slammed into his two companions. They all hit the ground. *Oof!*

Then all at once they were rolling down a hill, head over heels. When they finally came to a stop, they were in a valley. It was far below where they'd been only moments before. Far from that dog, thank goodness!

Poseidon's trident had wound up in Zeus's

lap. When Zeus sat up, the trident bumped the magical bolt tucked under his belt.

"Eware-bip the-Ip iver-Rip ethe-Lip," said a small, squeaky voice. It was Chip, Zeus's amulet! It spoke in Chip Latin, which was like Pig Latin, only you moved the first letter of each word to its end and added an "ip" sound in Chip Latin. Instead of the "ay" sound used in Pig Latin.

Poseidon looked over at Zeus, eyes wide. "Moldy mackerel! It's talking again?"

Excited, Zeus fished the amulet from the neck of his tunic and studied it. The symbols on it flickered briefly as he pushed the trident away. Then the amulet conked out again.

Disappointed, Zeus dropped the amulet back inside his tunic. "Guess not."

"But what did it say a minute ago?" asked

Poseidon. Zeus frowned uncertainly.

"Sounded like 'Beware the liver thief,'" said Hades.

"Well, that's a big help," said Poseidon. He picked up his trident, stood, and dusted himself off. Then he froze.

"You!" he blurted, staring at someone across the way. "Thanks for saving us the trouble of finding you again!"

Zeus and Hades scrambled to their feet to see who he was looking at.

Alongside a river that ran through the valley stood a familiar figure. A claw-handed Titan as tall as a tree.

"Oceanus," muttered Hades.

They'd captured Oceanus during their last quest, but he'd escaped before they could imprison him. Someday, somehow, they were going to have to lock all the Titan giants away.

Otherwise the Olympians would never be safe from them.

A woman with long dark red hair stood beside Oceanus. She, too, was as tall as a tree. Turning toward Oceanus, she gave him a metal bowl.

Grinning at the boys, Oceanus clacked one of his enormous claw hands at them in a taunting wave. Then, without a word, he dove into the river and swam away.

"Come back here, thief!" Poseidon shouted as the three boys rushed toward the river. He hadn't forgiven the Titan for stealing the trident from him long ago.

They'd all assumed that Oceanus had run off to King Cronus when he'd escaped them before. *Why did he come here instead?* Zeus wondered. *Who is this woman with him, and what are they up to?*

When the three boys reached the riverbank, they stared into the water where Oceanus had dived. This river was a clear, flowing blue. Very different from the River Styx. Zeus licked his lips, suddenly thirsty.

The red-haired woman still stood at the edge of the river. She seemed to be deep in thought. Suddenly she said, "I've got it! Roy G. Biv." She looked over at the boys. "What do you think?"

"About what?" Zeus looked up at her. And up, and up. "You're a Titan, aren't you?" he accused, before Poseidon or Hades could even open their mouths.

"Yes, I'm Mnemosyne," she replied, pronouncing it nuh-MAH-zuh-nee. "But fear not. I mean you no harm. Come, you boys look thirsty." It was like she'd read Zeus's mind!

She kneeled and dipped a tiny glass into the

river. In her fingers the glass looked as small as a thimble. When it was full, she held it out to the boys.

"Here, drink from my river," she told them. "Rest and forget your troubles awhile."

"Who's Roy G. Biv?" asked Poseidon. He stepped closer, reaching for the glass she offered. He took a drink.

"It's my new mnemonic," she explained easily. She pronounced the word as nuh-MAH-nick. "A mnemonic is a way of remembering something. For instance, 'Roy G. Biv' stands for the colors of a rainbow. Red, Orange, Yellow, Green, Blue, Indigo, Violet."

"Oh, I get it," said Hades.

Poseidon took another drink.

"My gift is the power of memory," she went on pleasantly. "That's how I came up with the idea for mnemonics like the one for the

rainbow. Down here the dead don't see many rainbows. I want to help them remember the colors."

Still kneeling, she dipped water from the river into two more glasses.

"We saw you talking to Oceanus," Zeus said. "What did he want?"

Mnemosyne shrugged, shifty-eyed. "Nothing much."

She smiled at Zeus and Hades. She held the two glasses of sparkling water out to them. "Drink," she crooned. "The waters of the River Lethe are the clearest of all five rivers in the Underworld. The most delicious, too. You'll forget any other water once you taste this."

Zeus was suspicious. But the sound of her voice and the sight of the water were making him thirstier than ever. He took the glass she offered. Beside him Hades took the other glass.

The River Lethe, thought Zeus. *Why does that ring a bell?* As he brought the glass to his lips, it clinked against his amulet. *That's it—the amulet!* he thought. *It had been trying to warn them about this river just a few minutes ago!*

He dropped his glass without drinking from it.

Thrusting out his hand, he slapped the glass from Hades' hands too, before he could drink.

Poseidon's glass was already half-empty. Still, Zeus leaped to Poseidon's side and swatted it away.

"Whoa! Why'd you do that?" Poseidon whined. "It was good."

"I just realized what Chip was trying to tell us before," exclaimed Zeus. "It said 'Beware the River Lethe'!"

Hades stepped back from the woman. "So you were trying to trick us!" he accused.

Mnemosyne laughed lightly and scooped two fresh glasses of water from the river. She tried to hand them to Zeus and Hades. "Don't be silly. Drink, Olympians," she ordered.

"What's an Olympian?" Poseidon asked blankly.

Zeus and Hades glanced at him in alarm.

"It's what, um, what *we* are!" Zeus told him. Mnemosyne didn't seem to realize that Zeus wasn't an Olympian like Poseidon and Hades. But that was probably a *good* thing.

She might fear him more if she didn't know he was only a mortal. Well, maybe he was a little more than a mortal. The oracle had called him a hero in training.

Looking determined, Mnemosyne rose to her feet. Zeus and Hades each grabbed one of Poseidon's arms. Then they skedaddled.

"Go ahead and run, little chicken boys!"

Mnemosyne yelled, not so nice anymore. "But if you think you'll escape us Titans this time—you can *forget* it!"

She let out a scary-sounding laugh. Then she dove into the river and swam away. Just as Oceanus had done.

Forget It

Am I a farmer?" Poseidon asked.

"A what?" asked Hades, giving him a weird look.

"A farmer," Poseidon said, studying the sharp prongs of his trident. "If not, why am I carrying around this pitchfork?"

Zeus frowned. "That's your trident. You're god of the sea. Don't you remember?"

After they'd escaped Mnemosyne, they'd

wound up here, walking through a smelly sulfur field surrounded by hot lava. Poseidon had been asking dumb questions nonstop. Ever since he'd drunk from that river.

"Oh, yeah. I remember now," said Poseidon. "I also remember that you're Zeus." He looked over at Hades. "But who are you? And I know that this is my left foot. But what do you call my other foot?"

Zeus snapped his fingers. "Right—I've figured it out!"

He leaned over to Hades, speaking quietly. "Poseidon drank *half* the water in the glass Mnemosyne gave him, remember? It must've made him forget *half* of everything."

"Great. Just when we need our wits about us, he turns into a half-wit," Hades murmured back. "He's not going to be any help in finding the helm now. Not as long as he's forgetting stuff."

Just then Poseidon laid his trident on the ground so he could pull a rock out of his sandal. When he started walking again, he left his trident behind, forgetting all about it.

Hades sent Zeus a *See what I mean?* glance.

Zeus picked up the trident and held it under one arm. It bumped his bolt dagger with every step. Before he could return the trident to Poseidon, the amulet around his neck suddenly twitched.

Excited, Zeus pulled the amulet out of his tunic with his free hand. A single word appeared on its surface in bold black letters: UNDERWORLD. When it faded away, some small words appeared on the amulet. There were lines too, some straight and others wavy.

"It's a map!" Zeus exclaimed.

Hades and Poseidon came over to look. "Of what?" Poseidon asked.

"I think it's the Underworld," Hades told him.

Zeus peered intently at Chip's surface. There were three areas circled on the map. Each was labeled with a letter. One had a *T*. One had an *E*. One had an *A*.

Under the *T* was the word, "Tartarus." Under the *E* were the words "Elysian Fields." Under the *A* was "Asphodel Meadow."

"Tartarus," Zeus mused. He looked up at his companions. "That's where the amulet told us to imprison Oceanus, when we were on our last quest. Looks like it's a place right here in the Underworld."

"So if we can recapture Oceanus, we could still take him there," said Hades. "Mnemosyne, too."

Poseidon pointed to the map. He moved his fingertip from the *T* to the *E* and on to the *A*. "That spells 'TEA'!"

"Or if you rearrange the letters they could spell 'EAT'!" Hades exclaimed. "Like those signs we saw before by the Underworld gates."

"Hey! I bet 'EAT' was another one of Mnemosyne's mnemonics," said Zeus. "To help people remember the layout of the Underworld. *E* for 'Elysian Fields,' *A* for 'Asphodel Meadow,' and *T* for 'Tartarus.'"

"So that's why the dog was making the shades form three lines?" asked Hades.

Zeus nodded. "Yeah, those must be the three places where the dead go."

"Okay, so I guess the dog doesn't eat the dead after all," said Hades. "But what if he eats the *living*? Like us!"

Poseidon was looking confused. "Dog?" he asked. "We have a dog? Awesome!" He glanced around as if searching for it. "Here, poochie, poochie."

"I'll be glad when he gets his memory back," said Hades. "*If* he ever does."

"Ditto," Zeus agreed. He handed the trident back to Poseidon. "Here, you forgot something. Don't let go of it again." The instant he handed over the trident, the words and lines on his amulet blinked out.

"Oh, no!" said Hades.

"Don't worry. I memorized the map," said Zeus. "Elysian Fields is closest, so let's check it out first. It's this way."

On the way to the fields, they explained to Poseidon about the quest they were on. Ten minutes later they were standing in front of a tall green hedge. There was a door in it with a sign that read:

WELCOME TO THE ELYSIAN FIELDS

WHERE EVERYONE IS GOOD, AND DEAD

They pushed the door open and went inside. The fields were beautiful, with grapevines, fruit trees, gardens, and sparkling fountains. There was a fancy glass greenhouse at the far side of a field of wildflowers. The boys didn't see any people, though.

Zeus sniffed the sweet smell in the air. "Mmm. Roses."

Poseidon plucked a bunch of plump grapes from one of the grapevines. As they moved through the fruit trees, Zeus picked an apple and Hades picked a pear. They all began munching.

"So this is where the good people go after they die," said Zeus. "Nice."

"Yeah, I could get used to it," said Poseidon.

Hades shrugged. "I guess. I prefer the smell of sulfur swamp myself."

Zeus tossed his apple core away and reached

toward a tree for another apple. Suddenly he noticed a long golden strand of hair caught on a low branch. He recalled Hera's long, golden hair whipping in the wind when some half-giants had chased them during their last quest.

"This looks like Hera's hair," he said. Poseidon and Hades studied the golden strand too.

"You think when she went looking for the trident, she wound up here?" asked Poseidon.

It was weird, the stuff he could remember, when he forgot everything else. But at least he could remember Hera.

Suddenly they heard a girl's voice call out, "Help!"

Zeus gasped. "Was that Hera? Sounds like she's in trouble!"

"Hey! There's Oceanus," said Hades.

Sure enough, Oceanus was across the field of flowers now. It looked like he was locking the greenhouse. Was there someone imprisoned inside it. Hera, maybe?

Without thinking, Zeus whipped out his dagger-size thunderbolt. "Large!" he commanded. Nothing happened. The bolt didn't get big or spark with electricity. He'd forgotten it had no powers here in the Underworld. So why had Chip worked briefly before, he wondered.

"The three of us can take him," said Hades. "Even without magic."

"We have to try, anyway," said Poseidon.

Zeus tucked the bolt back into his belt. "Give us Hera!" he shouted to Oceanus.

"Make me!" Oceanus yelled back.

The three boys charged toward him across the field. They drew closer and closer. But right before they reached him, Oceanus disappeared into thin air!

CHAPTER SIX

The Helm

The minute Oceanus disappeared, Mnemosyne suddenly appeared a few feet away. She sprang into action. "Nyah, nyah. You can't catch me!" Her giant footsteps took her in another direction, away from the boys.

"They've got magic," said Zeus.

Poseidon nodded. "Magic that works in this world."

"Let's get her!" shouted Hades. The three boys rushed toward the orchard where Mnemosyne now stood.

Right before they reached her, she went invisible too! And then Oceanus reappeared. He ran over by the grapevines.

This appearing and disappearing happened over and over. Just when the boys thought they'd cornered one of the Titans, he or she vanished. Then the other Titan appeared nearby to tease and laugh at them.

When they charged Mnemosyne yet again, she was standing in front of a stone wall. Suddenly a bowl appeared in her hands. Quickly she put it on her head. Then she disappeared.

The boys couldn't stop in time. *Bam!* They crashed into the wall.

"Ow!"

"Ow!"

"Ow!"

Zeus sat up, rubbing the lump he'd gotten when his head hit the wall. "What's going on here? Why do we only see one of them at a time?"

"They must have something magic that's making them invisible," said Poseidon. "Maybe it's that metal bowl they keep passing between them."

"That's not a bowl," argued Hades. "It's a hat. Or a helmet. Why else would they keep putting it on top of their heads?"

"Wait! That's it!" said Zeus. "It's a helmet. As in '*helm.*' Get it?"

"That's right, fools!" said Mnemosyne. Though she was still invisible, she had obviously overheard them. "We are in possession of the Helm of Darkness." She laughed in that scary way again.

"Stole it from the throne of the lord of the Underworld himself!" Oceanus bragged. He was standing far across the field of wildflowers. It was as if he were afraid to come closer.

The boys huddled up to talk. "Why don't they attack us?" Zeus whispered.

"I think they're scared of your weapons," said Hades. "Of the magic in your bolt and Poseidon's trident."

"My trident is magic?" said Poseidon. He stared at it in awe.

Zeus rolled his eyes. He'd forgotten for a minute that Poseidon couldn't remember a lot of stuff. But maybe Hades was onto something.

"I bet you're right," Zeus told Hades. "I mean, that helm's magic seems to work fine in the Underworld. So maybe they haven't guessed that our magic *doesn't*."

"So let's pretend like it does work," Hades suggested.

"Yeah, maybe the Titans will fall for it," said Poseidon.

"Good plan," agreed Zeus. When they broke out of the huddle, he and Poseidon pulled out their weapons. They waved them menacingly over their heads.

Hades stood between them as they all confronted the Titans. "Give us the Helm of Darkness!" he commanded.

Oceanus eyed Poseidon's trident, turning pale. *Clackety-clack!* His claw hands clacked together nervously. He backed away. Then he ran to the far end of the hedge, leaped over it, and escaped.

"Wait for me!" shouted Mnemosyne. They couldn't see her, but they saw the tall flowers part in the field as she ran away. Seconds later they heard the two Titans arguing in the distance.

"It worked!" said Poseidon, punching his fist in the air. "They didn't guess that our weapons are temporarily powerless!"

"Help! Let me out of here," called a girl's muffled voice.

"Hera!" said Zeus. "She must be inside that greenhouse. C'mon. Let's rescue her."

"You and Poseidon can do that," said Hades. "I'll go after the helm." He turned toward the hedge.

Zeus grabbed his arm, stopping him. "No splitting up! That's how we lost Hera in the first place. I say we save her first. Then we'll all go after the helm together."

"Okay, fine," huffed Hades, sounding a little annoyed.

The three boys ran for the greenhouse.

Through its glass walls they could see that there was a girl inside. She was about their same age. But she wasn't Hera. There were flower blossoms in her light red hair, and she was wearing a flowing green dress.

"Who are you?" Zeus and Poseidon called through the glass to her at the same time.

"Demeter!" said Hades, grinning. He looked at Poseidon. "We grew up with her. All of us in King Cronus's belly. Then Zeus freed us. Remember?"

Poseidon shook his head. "Nuh-uh."

Hades reached for the greenhouse doorknob. "Ignore Poseidon," he called through the glass to Demeter. "He drank from the River Lethe. Lost half his memory."

"Oh, no!" she said, staring at them through the glass.

Poseidon looked a little embarrassed.

"It's locked," Hades announced when the

door wouldn't open. "Stand back, Demeter. We'll break the glass."

"You can't," Demeter told them. "Hera was imprisoned with me for a while, and we tried to break it. But it's magic. Unbreakable. So don't waste your time. Go after Hera." She made a shooing motion with her hand. "And then come back for me. She's in the Underworld too, trapped in Asphodel Meadow."

"Okay," said Hades. "We'll be back in a—"

"We'll set Demeter free first," Zeus insisted, cutting him off. "Then we'll search for Hera together."

Demeter smiled at him. "Hera told me you were a bossy thunderpants," she said teasingly.

Now it was Zeus's turn to look embarrassed. He hadn't minded when Hera had called him Thunderboy. But her other nicknames for him stunk worse than the River Styx!

"How'd you wind up here?" Zeus asked her, to change the subject. Meanwhile Poseidon began poking the lock with one of the sharp tips of his trident, trying to pick it.

"Mnemosyne brought me here on King Cronus's orders. She and Oceanus planned to take both Hera and me to a more secure hiding place today. To Tartarus." She shivered. "It's the lowest, foulest pit in the Underworld."

Just then the lock gave. Demeter shot out of the greenhouse door. "Come on," she called, making for the hedge. "To Asphodel Meadow!"

The four of them dashed through the hedge door and out of the Elysian Fields. Then Demeter stopped short, looking around. "Unfortunately, I don't know exactly where Asphodel Meadow is," she admitted.

"I do," said Zeus. "I saw a map." He took the lead, knowing it probably made him look bossy again. But sometimes the urge to take charge like this came over him. It was happening more and more as the days passed.

Ten minutes later the four of them came to a huge meadow of star-shaped white flowers.

"Wow! This must be what snow looks like," said Hades. Since the Olympians had been trapped in King Cronus's belly their whole lives, they'd never seen snow.

"It's asphodel," Demeter informed them. "The only flower that will grow in the Underworld outside of the Elysian Fields."

"Look—the Titans. They have Hera!" said Poseidon, gesturing across the meadow.

Sure enough, Oceanus and Mnemosyne were both visible now. Oceanus was carrying Hera. Mnemosyne was holding the helm.

"Hmm. That helm must only make you invisible if it's on your head," Zeus told the others.

Roarrr! Roarrr! Roarrr!

At the sudden sound the boys and Demeter whipped around in surprise. Behind them the enormous slobbering three-headed dog was headed their way, looking ready to pounce.

"Run for your lives!" yelled Hades. The four of them took off across the meadow, racing in different directions. The Titans laughed, apparently enjoying their fright.

The dog charged after Hades. Easily catching up, it frolicked around him in happy circles. Its three heads licked him, like Hades and the dog were long-lost best friends.

"Ick! Get away!" said Hades, swatting at the dog as he ran. Surprise—it didn't listen. "Fetch," he ordered desperately. He pointed toward the Titans.

Looking thrilled to have been given a job to do, the dog bounded across the meadow.

When it returned, it held Hera in one of its mouths.

There was also one Titan in each of its other mouths. Only a dog like this—one nearly as big as a temple—could manage such a feat!

All three captives were protesting loudly. The dragon dog dropped them at Hades' feet, like it was bringing him roadkill. The helm slipped from Mnemosyne's clutches as she tumbled to the ground. The magical object rolled toward Hades. It was almost as big as he was!

"Whoa!" he said, backing away. Before he could run, it bumped into him, knocking him over. In the blink of an eye, it shrank down to a size that would fit the head of a boy.

And for just a second Hades thought the helm flashed with gold and jewels! He blinked. When he looked again, he saw only a plain old spiked helmet. He must have been imagining things.

As Hades was getting to his feet, Zeus and Poseidon reached his side.

Poseidon snatched up the helm. He put it on his head and turned invisible. "We have the helm," his voice said gleefully.

CHAPTER SEVEN

The Furies

Hera jumped to her feet and wiped at her arms. "Eew! Dog slobber," she complained.

"Hera!" Demeter squealed joyfully.

"Demeter!" Hera squealed back. The two girls threw their arms around each other and hugged.

"Hera!" Still invisible, Poseidon wrapped his arms around both girls, making it a three-way hug. Since he only recalled half of everything, Zeus figured it made sense that he'd remember Hera, even if he'd forgotten Demeter.

But Poseidon also seemed to have forgotten how annoying he'd always considered Hera. That could be a good thing, though. Maybe there'd be fewer arguments between them.

Meanwhile, the Titans tried to sneak away. The dog was watching and quickly nabbed them again. Then it pinned them to the ground with its front paws. It grinned over at Hades, and made that happy gurgle sound again. "Sir. Brr. Us."

Though wary of the dog, the others gathered near it. After the boys explained to the girls about the oracle sending them on this quest for the helm, they made plans.

"I say we imprison these two Titans in Tartarus first thing," said Hera. Demeter nodded.

"Sounds good," said Hades. "After that we can look for the lord of the Underworld and return the helm to him."

"Or *her*," Hera put in.

"Come on, then," said Poseidon's disembodied voice. "Zeus knows the way."

"Of course he does," said Hera, rolling her eyes.

"You're welcome," Zeus huffed in reply as they all began walking. By now she'd hugged everyone but him. He was feeling left out. Not that he actually *wanted* a hug, of course.

"For what?" she asked, frowning over at him. "Saving me? Humph! I could've saved myself. Without the slobber."

"Where've you been, anyway?" Hades asked her.

"I got caught in an ocean current while looking for the trident," she explained. "Oceanus's doing. It swept me from sea to sea until I wound up in the River Styx. I've been trapped in the Underworld ever since."

As the group headed out of Asphodel Meadow, Zeus and Poseidon took the lead. Hera and Demeter were behind them, chatting away. Poseidon had given them the helm, and they were trying it on and giggling at being invisible.

Last of all came Hades and the dragon dog. The pooch carried Mnemosyne and Oceanus in its jaws like the two Titans were oversize dog toys.

"Go away. . . . Don't walk so close to me. . . . Stop breathing on me," Hades ordered now and then. But the dog just kept gazing at him with adoring puppy-dog eyes.

Every so often the Titans would start complaining, asking to be put down. But with a hard shake of his heads, the dog would shut them up.

A feeling of satisfaction settled over Zeus. "Four Olympians down, one to go," he said to Poseidon as they walked. "Only Hestia is still missing."

"You mean *five* Olympians down, right?" said Poseidon. "Including you."

Zeus's brow wrinkled in confusion. "Huh?" What was he talking about? Zeus was no Olympian! Thinking that Poseidon's memory was still half cuckoo from his River Lethe drink, Zeus decided to let the comment pass.

Just then Hera called to Poseidon, asking about his trident. For some reason, she eyed Zeus a little nervously.

Poseidon dropped back and proudly showed the trident off to the girls. "I'm god of the sea," he bragged to them.

Zeus couldn't help feeling a little jealous. Someday he'd have to give up his thunderbolt to that Goose guy it belonged to. But Poseidon would get to keep his trident forever.

As they all approached the dreaded pit of the Underworld—Tartarus—Hera accidentally dropped the helm.

"Careful," Zeus cautioned. "That helm's got powerful magic."

"Okay, Mr. Bossy Bolts," she told him. "You carry it. It's heavy." She tossed the helm to him and he caught it.

At the exact same time the dragon dog suddenly spit out the two Titans. *Patooey! Patooey!* It started barking wildly.

The Titans scrambled to their feet, ready to run for it. But Poseidon and Zeus drew their trident and thunderbolt, keeping them in check.

"What is that weird dog of yours barking at?" Poseidon asked Hades.

"It's not mine!" Hades said quickly. One of

the dog's heads stopped barking long enough to reach over and give Hades a lick, as if to say, *Of course I am.*

"Well, he sure has taken a licking—I mean, a liking—to you," teased Hera.

"Ha-ha," grumped Hades.

"Hey! What are those?" asked Demeter. She pointed upward. Three winged creatures were flying above them!

Mnemosyne squinted at them, then paled. "Oh, no! It's the Furies."

"Is that bad?" asked Hera.

"They're Creatures of Chaos!" Oceanus bellowed. "Of course it's bad."

As the Furies flew closer, Zeus saw they were women. One had a long pointy nose, another wore black pointy boots, and the third one had pointed ears. All three had wild hair and wore long black dresses. The belts and bracelets they had on were woven of live snakes!

The Furies circled overhead, gazing suspiciously down at the group on the ground. Finally each of them screeched out a question.

"Who goes there?"

"Why are you here?"

"What do you want?"

"We're Olympians!" Hades replied.

"We're taking prisoners to Tartarus," Hera added.

"We don't want any trouble," Zeus said in answer to the third question. He was hoping he could reason with them.

That had been impossible with the Androphagoi, the last Creatures of Chaos they'd tangled with. They'd had mouths in the middle of their chests and sharp, bone-crunching teeth. Brandishing clubs and spears, they'd attacked without asking any questions.

But it seemed that the Furies weren't interested in reason either. When they noticed the helm in Zeus's hands, they chorused furiously, "Thieves! You have stolen the helm. You must be punished!"

All at once the winged women dive-bombed them. Everyone started to run.

"Do something! Use your thunderbolt," Hera urged Zeus.

"Its magic doesn't work in the Underworld," Poseidon called back, without thinking.

Hearing this, the two Titans looked at each other. Then Zeus saw them look at the helm. It must be more powerful than anyone knew, since they wanted it so badly. Badly enough to stick around in hopes of surviving the Furies and stealing it back.

Luckily, the dragon dog's three heads were keeping the Furies at bay by snapping at them. For now at least.

"Leave us alone!" Zeus hollered to the Furies as he ran. "The Titans stole the Helm of Darkness. Not us."

Mnemosyne got a crafty look on her face. "They're lying! These five spawns of evil came here on a quest to steal the helm. Right, Oceanus?"

Oceanus hesitated, then nodded. He wasn't all bad, Zeus knew. But he was easily influenced by the other Titans, especially King Cronus. And apparently by Mnemosyne, too.

Mnemosyne jabbered on to the Furies, telling lies. "In fact, we saw them steal it. From the jeweled box on the throne that awaits the true lord of the Underworld."

"No! We're innocent," said Demeter.

Confounded, the Furies flew around and around the group.

"If someone doesn't confess, we'll drive you all into a river of lava," Pointy-Boots threatened.

"No! I say we dump them all in a sulfur swamp," said Pointy-Ears.

"I say we put a pox on them," said Pointy-Nose. She drew back and hurled what looked like a handful of beans at them.

They struck the dragon dog. Immediately it began scratching. She'd hit it with a pox of fleas!

"Idiot! You missed," Pointy-Boots complained.

"Did not."

"Did too. You should have hit the thieves, not their dog."

And with that the three Furies began fighting among themselves. They whipped their snakes around, clawing at one another.

"See?" Hades panted to Zeus as they continued to run. "This is why I liked it in Cronus's belly. No Creatures of Chaos. No Titans. No trouble. But then you had to come along and free us."

"It was a prison!" said Zeus.

"It was better than being chased by Furies," insisted Hades.

"True," Poseidon agreed. "In the king's belly we only had to dodge the occasional fish bone or incoming Olympian. I'm still glad we're out, though."

"Well, I'm not." Hades frowned at Zeus. "And Hera's right. You *are* bossy!"

And just like that, the boys started fighting too.

CHAPTER EIGHT

Tag! You're Dead.

"Stop it, you dweebs!" Hera yelled at the three boys.

But the Furies' anger seemed to have infected them. The boys began throwing punches. Poseidon swung his trident. Zeus drew his bolt. Hades snatched the helm from Zeus and slung it at the other two.

As they all struck out at the same time, the three objects they held connected. *Zap! Fizz! Zing!*

Suddenly the thunderbolt sparked with wild electricity. The spark spread to the trident and then the helm. All three began to glow with a magical golden light. Then the helm transformed before Hades' eyes, flashing with jewels. He dropped it like a hot potato.

Surprised, the boys jumped apart. Instantly the spark of magic faded.

"What just happened?" Hades wondered.

"Yeah, I thought you said your weapons' magic didn't work in the Underworld," said Demeter.

"It didn't. Until now," said Poseidon. "When they touched."

Before Hades could grab the helm from the ground, the dog dashed over and made off with it. No one else seemed to have noticed the flash of jewels, Hades realized. And the jewels were gone now. What was going on here?

"It may have been magic, but it was weak," said Zeus. "Not powerful enough to defeat those Furies."

"Well, that's really too bad," said Hera, pointing upward. "Because they've stopped fighting now. And it looks like they're coming in for the kill!"

Zeus, the Olympians, and the dog took off running again. They were right behind the Titans.

Sulfur smoke was all around them now. The pit of Tartarus lay dead ahead. The Furies were herding them into it! But at the last second the winged creatures backed off, circling overhead again. Zeus and the others stopped on the brink of the pit, huddling together.

"We have decided to give you a task as punishment," announced Pointy-Boots.

"Evildoers always fail at our tasks," said Pointy-Nose.

Pointy-Ears nodded. "So we'll figure out who's lying soon enough."

"I'll choose the task," said Pointy-Nose. "I'm very creative when it comes to punishments. Remember the time I put a pox on—"

"Ack! I'm the creative one," interrupted Pointy-Boots. "Remember the never-ending task of sorting asphodel seeds I gave those shades last month? Now *that* was creative!"

"It's nothing compared to what I did to those troublemaking shades last week," insisted Pointy-Ears. "Making them balance for hours on their heads and say tongue twisters while I tickled their feet with a feather? Classic."

Their captives listened in horror.

"I feel kind of woozy," said Demeter.

"Me too," said Poseidon.

Zeus stared into the pit of Tartarus. "I think

it's the stinky sulfur fumes coming from down there."

Oceanus nodded, and Mnemosyne fanned her nose.

"I like the stink," said Hades. "It helps me think. And here's what I'm thinking now: Since those Furies are trying to one-up one another with punishment ideas, I say we give them an idea of our own."

He winked at Zeus. Then he said extra loudly, "I hope the Furies don't choose a game as our task. Games terrify me. Especially a game like, um—"

"Tag?" suggested Zeus.

"Right," said Hades. Then he hissed at the others, "C'mon. Pretend you're scared of tag."

"Oh, no! Not a game of tag!" wailed Hera, catching on.

She elbowed Poseidon, prompting him to add, "Um, yeah, not tag!"

"Please, we beg of you," Demeter shouted. "Anything but that!"

As the Furies gathered to whisper together in midair, the Titans didn't speak. But the two of them were looking mighty nervous.

Then the Furies began to fly in circles again. Pointy-Boots peered down at all of them. "We have decided your punishment!" she proclaimed. "You must survive a game of tag. With Thanatos."

"Doesn't sound bad," Hera murmured.

"Yeah, I'm good at tag," Demeter whispered back.

Zeus nodded. "Me too." He'd outrun hundreds of thunderbolts back home on the Greek island of Crete. For some reason, until he'd gotten Bolt, thunderbolts had always been out to get him.

"This'll be a cinch," Poseidon added.

"You think so?" scoffed Mnemosyne.

Watching the three Furies still circling high overhead, she looked terrified.

She must know something that the rest of us don't, thought Zeus. It didn't take long to find out what that was.

Suddenly the Furies chanted: "Come forth, Thanatos, Bringer of Death!"

Zeus, the Titans, and his companions all looked at one another. That did not sound good.

"I have come!" boomed a voice in immediate reply. A man appeared from the gloom overhead and slowly sank to the ground.

No taller than a mortal man, he wore a billowing cape as gray as fog. Its hood hung low on his head, so you couldn't see his face. Except for his eerie smile.

Thanatos bowed to the Furies. "Ladies, I'm honored you have chosen me to execute this punishment. He grinned. And I *do* mean execute.

There's nothing I like better than a game of Tag! You're Dead." He rubbed his hands together and scanned his victims.

Zeus gulped. "You mean if you tag us, we fall down dead? Really and truly dead? Never-leave-the-Underworld-again dead?"

"You got it," said Thanatos. That creepy smile of his got even wider. He whipped his arms high and began whirling in a circle. This sent a gust of wind whooshing their way. It blew all seven of them—and the dog—into the pit of Tartarus.

And then they were falling. Not at normal speed but in slow motion, like they were in a dream. Or more like a nightmare. They went deeper and deeper and deeper.

When they landed at the bottom of the pit, the dragon dog dropped the helm. Before Hades could grab it, the dog snatched it up again and galloped off.

"Come back here, you crazy dragon dog!" he called. The smell of sulfur was thick around them. It seemed to have killed off the fleas. But though the dog had stopped scratching, it was too busy investigating everything to obey orders. And it still had the helm in its jaws.

Just then Thanatos dropped down into the pit too. When his feet touched the ground, he spoke to them in his eerie voice. "Game's on! Better start running."

And with that, the most terrifying game of tag ever played began. Thanatos was "it" and he chased them all, swooping and diving.

The Olympians and Titans slipped and slid in ooky globs of swampy stuff, trying to get away from him. Tartarus was even gloomier and stinkier than all they'd seen before in the Underworld. No flowers, trees, or plants grew here. Their only hiding places were behind sharp obsidian rocks that jutted from the ground like tombstones.

And the dog was no help to them. He kept bounding around the pit, acting like he thought this new game was all in fun.

The three boys and two girls spread out, each taking cover as best they could. So did the Titans.

"Thanatos is toying with us," Zeus told Hades as he ran past him. "I'm sure he's hoping we'll get tired sooner or later. Then he'll move in for the tag—er, kill."

A few minutes later Hades spotted Hera a dozen feet away. She was crouched behind a lava rock. Thanatos was sneaking up on her, looking like he meant business.

"Run, Hera!" Hades cried out.

Thanatos whipped around. Hera escaped. But now Thanatos set his sights on Hades instead.

Feeling powerless to help, Zeus watched Hades face off against the hooded Death guy. Slowly Hades was forced into a corner between two large hunks of rock.

"Back off," Hades told Thanatos. But the tremor in his voice betrayed his fear.

Grinning, the Bringer of Death crept closer. His long gray fingers reached out. They came closer. And closer. Until a gray fingertip was only an inch away from Hades' cheek.

"Tag," Thanatos whispered softly. "You're—"

CHAPTER NINE

Lord of the Underworld

But Thanatos never got to finish saying, *You're dead.*

Just as he was about to tag Hades, the dog made that gurgle again. "Sir. Brr. Us." He jerked his chin up, flinging the helm in a high arc through the air.

Hades stretched out his arm and grabbed the helm as it zoomed by. The moment he touched it, the helm transformed into a dazzling jeweled crown!

Seeing this, Thanatos stopped dead still. So did Hades. So did everyone else. They all stared at the crown in amazement.

So I wasn't imagining the flash of gold and jewels when I touched the helm before, thought Hades. Quickly he set the crown on top of his head. "Am I invisible?"

"Yes!" Zeus called to him.

As the Olympians and Titans gathered around, Thanatos bowed low to Hades. That is, to the empty spot where he'd just been standing. "All hail the lord of the Underworld!"

"Who, me?" Hades' voice asked in surprise. Thanatos nodded.

Hades removed the helm and examined it.

It remained golden and jeweled. He set it on a rock. It turned back into a plain helmet. He picked it up again. Crown.

"So that's why that dog likes you," said Hera. "You're the lord of the Underworld!"

"And that must be why the sulfur in this world makes you think better," added Zeus.

"And why you like stink," Poseidon added.

"I am your servant," Thanatos said humbly to Hades. "What would you bid me do?"

"How about you call off this game?" Hades suggested. He put the helm crown on again, going invisible.

The crown, the invisibility, and the knowledge that he was lord of the Underworld seemed to make him feel suddenly powerful. "And keep your fog fingers off my friends from now on," he added.

"Yeah," said Zeus. To show support he and

Poseidon came up to stand on either side of Hades. (At least they thought they were probably on either side of him.) Hera and Demeter joined them.

"Your wish is my command, O lord of the Underworld," said Thanatos.

Just then the Furies appeared overhead. They flew above the group in the pit like vultures circling their prey.

"Lord of the Underworld? No way! They have tricked you, Thanatos," said Pointy-Ears.

"You're wrong," Thanatos replied. "The invisible boy is the one we've awaited—the true lord of this world!"

Hades took the helm off, showing them the fabulous crown it became in his hands.

"It's just some sort of magic spell," said Pointy-Boots.

"Punishment must be served," added Pointy-Nose.

The Furies zoomed on the currents of sulfurous air, cackling and loudly flapping their wings.

"Duck! They're going to attack!" yelled Hera.

Hades thrust his arm up, holding the helm high. "Zeus, draw your bolt," he commanded. "Poseidon, hold up your trident."

"What about us?" Hera asked.

"Yeah," said Demeter. "What should we do?"

"Um . . . slap hands with us," Hades told her. "Now let's high-five!"

At his command five hands (three of them holding powerful, magical objects) touched as one. *Zap! Fizz! Zing! Slap! Slap!*

Instantly the bolt, trident, and helm all sizzled with a tremendous power the likes of which they'd never before seen.

"Flippin' fish sticks!" Poseidon yelled.

"Helmtastic!" cheered Hades.

"Thunderation!" exclaimed Zeus.

"Amazing!" Hera shouted.

"Awesome!" said Demeter.

The five of them broke apart, staring breathlessly at one another. Stunned by this display of power, Mnemosyne and Oceanus cringed in fear. Even the circling Furies now seemed impressed.

"What just happened?" asked Hades.

"Teamwork," Mnemosyne pronounced in an awed tone. "Your magic. It's bolstered through the power of teamwork."

"It appears that these Olympians are even stronger than King Cronus feared," Oceanus murmured to her.

"Strong enough that they overcame the Underworld's resistance to Earth magic," said Thanatos, sounding impressed. "Normally the sulfur here drains away the power of all magic that enters the Underworld from the Earth realm. Prevents shades from sneaking in magical weapons."

Pointing toward the Furies, Hades shouted a bold command to the Titans. "Tell them the truth. Tell them you were lying before."

Mnemosyne and Oceanus looked at each other. Then Oceanus shrugged and gazed up at the Furies. "All right. We admit it. *We* stole the helm."

The Furies gasped. In awe of Hades now, they fell all over themselves trying to please him.

"Oh, let me be the one to punish the Titans for stealing your crown, lord of the Underworld," begged Pointy-Boots. "If it is your wish, I can peck out the eyes of these thieves in less than three seconds."

"I can scratch them to ribbons in two seconds," Pointy-Ears put in quickly.

"That's nothing! In one second I can give them a pox that will make them itch as if bitten by a thousand fire ants!" claimed Pointy-Nose.

Yet another pox, thought Zeus. *Must be her specialty.*

"Uh, okay, good to know," Hades told them. "For now, though, maybe you could just stick these two Titans someplace secure in Tartarus. Someplace they will never escape from."

The Furies gleefully carried out his orders, herding Mnemosyne and Oceanus off. After they were gone, everything got quiet.

"Now what?" asked Hera.

"We go back to Earth," said Zeus.

"How?" asked Poseidon.

"Allow me to assist," said Thanatos.

Zeus looked over, surprised to see he was still there.

Thanatos clapped his pale hands together.

Whoosh! A chariot drawn by four black horses appeared alongside them. The group of five quickly boarded it.

"Upon your return to the Underworld one day in the future, we will hold a coronation ceremony and show you to your throne," Thanatos told Hades.

"Throne?" Hera echoed. "He gets a crown *and* a throne?"

"Well, he *is* lord of the Underworld," Thanatos told her. "And that's what the god of this world is supposed to get."

"I guess," Hera said, pouting.

Hades bid farewell to Thanatos, who was staying behind. Then he patted the dragon dog on each of its three heads in turn.

"Sir. Brr. Us," the dog gurgled happily.

"I think I'll name you Cerberus," Hades told the dog. "Since that's what you're always saying.

And since it looks like you're going to be mine after all. What do you think, boy?"

The dog licked Hades' face with all three of his tongues.

"I think he likes it," Demeter teased.

Hades smiled. "Be a good boy, Cerberus. Thanatos will take you out of the pit. And I'll come back soon."

Then Hades called to the horses. "Away!" he commanded. And just like that, the chariot lifted off.

"Hey, I just thought of a joke Charon would love," Hades announced as they began to rise. "Why did the chariot wheel come loose?" Then he supplied the answer before anyone could guess. "Because it needed to be *Titaned*."

Laughter filled the chariot as it took them higher. Soon they were out of the pit of Tartarus.

Only a thick layer of dirt and rock overhead separated them from the surface of the Earth above. But as they approached the rock full speed, the chariot didn't slow.

"Stop! We're going to crash!" Zeus yelled as they rose perilously close. Some of the others gasped or screamed.

Crack! A hole magically opened in the layer of dirt and rock above them. The chariot cut through it. They were out of the Underworld!

They touched down safely on the hill overlooking the River Styx. Right where the boys' journey had begun that very morning.

The minute they all stepped down from the chariot, two things happened. The horse-drawn chariot headed back to Tartarus. And Poseidon's memory returned.

"Right foot. Left foot! I remember everything again!" he said in a delighted voice. As his words died away, a cloud of glittery mist appeared before them.

"Pythia!" Zeus exclaimed.

Demeter gaped as a face framed by long black hair appeared within the mist.

"Oracle," Hera told her before she could ask questions. "I'll explain later."

CHAPTER TEN

Olympians, One and tw

The oracle's face glowed within the mist. She blinked as she took off her fogged glasses to polish them. Then she put them back on.

"Congratulations, Demeter, Hades, Hera, Poseidon, and Zeus." The oracle smiled at each of them in turn as she spoke their names. "You have succeeded in your quest. The Helm of Darkness is now in the right hands."

the right head," said Hades'

Zeus looked around. Where was he? Then Hades reappeared behind him, holding the jeweled helm. He'd slipped it on for fun.

Pythia gave him a slight bow. "I hail you, lord of the Underworld. It is good and just that you have regained your rightful throne."

"Wish *I* had a throne," said Poseidon. He sounded a bit jealous. Zeus understood since he'd sometimes felt the same way about Poseidon's trident.

"At least you've got a trident," Hera shot back. She sounded a little jealous too. "I've got nothing. Neither does Demeter." She looked at the oracle. "Will I ever get a magical object like Zeus's bolt. Or Poseidon's trident? Or Hades' helm?"

Before Pythia could think them ungrateful for what they *did* have, and for the help she'd given them so far, Zeus chimed in, "We're grateful to you for guiding us in our quests. But before you give us a new one, we have a few things we'd like to ask."

"Very well. I will allow questions," said the oracle. "But you may ask only three."

"Why only three?" asked Poseidon.

"Because three is the most magical number of things," Pythia said matter-of-factly. As if that should've been obvious.

"Please don't make that the first question you answered," Hera begged the oracle.

Pythia smiled. "I won't."

Phew, thought Zeus. He kneeled and picked five blades of grass. Three were long and two were short. He stood again and held them in his fist out to the others. "Longs get to ask a question," he said.

Luckily, he picked one of the long blades. So did Hera and Poseidon.

"Will Demeter and I ever get our own magical objects?" Hera asked, going first.

"Yes. In time," promised the oracle.

"What will mine be?" Hera asked eagerly. The oracle did not reply.

"You only get one question!" Poseidon reminded her. Looked like those two were back to bickering now that Poseidon's memory had returned, thought Zeus.

Quickly Poseidon asked the second question. "What do you see in our future?"

"The future is what you make of it," Pythia replied. "But dark forces are gathering. You must be strong. As one. A team. If and when all of the Olympians are united again, you will have the power to defeat Cronus and his evil ways. If you fail, the entire world will be lost to chaos and destruction."

"But, hey—no pressure, right?" Poseidon joked lamely.

No one laughed. From the grim set of his jaw, even Poseidon seemed to realize that the idea of a world lost to chaos wasn't a funny one.

Pythia glanced at Zeus since it was his turn now. He opened his mouth. He'd planned to ask about his parents. He really had. But for some reason another question fell from his lips instead. "Am I an Olympian like the others, or am I a hero in training?"

At this, the mist around the oracle seemed to glow more brightly. "You are both," she said gently.

"Sorry, I should've told you that you were an Olympian," said Hera. "I kept it a secret for too long. I wanted to make sure you were on our side."

Zeus had little time to consider all this before Pythia spoke again. "And now begins a new quest," she told them all briskly. "Next you must find the Olympic Torch, which rightfully belongs to the Protector of the Hearth.

"Find the torch, and you will also find more of those you seek. Only, you must go carefully. For with each of your successes, King Cronus fears you more. And I fear for *you* when you next come upon him. It will be soon. Beware . . ."

With that, the oracle faded from view. They were all silent for a minute, watching the magical glittering mist until it disappeared.

Then Zeus raised his thunderbolt high. He pointed it westward, and everyone looked in that direction. The sun was setting there in the

distance, on the horizon. The sky was so orange and pink that it almost appeared to be on fire.

"Onward," he called out in a clear, brave voice. "To adventure."

Poseidon raised his trident. Hades raised his helm. Hera and Demeter raised their hands. They all touched, doing a high-five that excited their magic again.

Zap! Fizz! Zing! Slap! Slap!

"Onward!" they shouted as one. Then they turned to head toward the horizon.

Whoosh! Suddenly a giant fireball soared through the sky overhead. It screamed downward, heading right for them!

"Take cover!" yelled Zeus. Everyone spread out, running. He leaped behind a boulder just in the nick of time.

Ka-BOOM! The fireball exploded as it hit the earth.

As the smoke and dust cleared, Zeus peeked out. His eyes widened when he saw what had happened. There was now a crater in the exact spot where he'd been standing only seconds ago. The remains of the red-hot fireball still sizzled inside it.

Had the ball of fire been sent here on purpose to blow him to smithereens? By who? He didn't know. But one thing he did know. He was going to find out!

Join Zeus and his friends as they set off on the adventure of a lifetime.

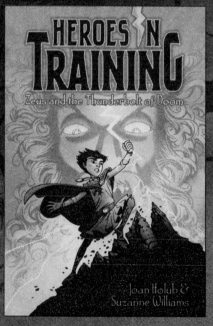

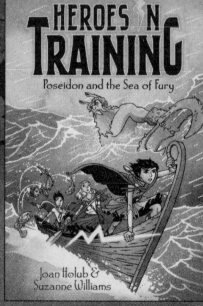